The Flying Canoe

A CHRISTMAS STORY

retold by ERIC A. KIMMEL

illustrated by DANIEL SAN SOUCI

and JUSTIN SAN SOUCI

Holiday House / New York

Text copyright © 2011 by Eric A. Kimmel
Illustrations copyright © 2011 by Daniel San Souci and Justin San Souci
All Rights Reserved
HOLIDAY HOUSE is registered in the U.S. Patent and Trademark Office.
Printed and Bound in April 2011 at Kwong Fat Offset Printing Co., Ltd.,
Dongguan City, China.
The text typeface is Cheltenham BT.
The artwork was created with traditional and digital media.
www.holidayhouse.com
First Edition

Library of Congress Cataloging-in-Publication Data
Kimmel, Eric A.
The Flying Canoe : a Christmas story / retold by Eric A. Kimmel ;
illustrated by Daniel San Souci and Justin San Souci.
p. cm.
Summary: On Christmas Eve, six French-Canadian trappers meet a mysterious stranger
who gives them the gift of a trip to their homes in Montreal, if only they agree
not to speak until they cross their own thresholds.
ISBN 0-8234-1730-1 (hardcover)
[1. Christmas—Folklore. 2. French Canadians—Folklore.
3. Folklore—Canada.]
I. Title: Chasse-Gallérie. II. San Souci, Daniel, ill. III. Title.
PZ8.1.K567 Fl 2011
398.2—dc21
[E]
2002033936

ISBN-13: 978-0-8234-1730-8

One Christmas Eve six French fur traders huddled around a campfire in the frozen woods beyond Lake Nipigon in Ontario. They did not wish one another *"Joyeux Noël."* There was precious little to celebrate in that camp. They were cold, hungry, and far away from their homes and families.

"In Montréal they will be going to church soon," said Pierre.

"They are finishing a fine Christmas dinner," Étienne added.

"If I close my eyes I can smell roast goose." Pascal sighed.

"And ham. And more *tartes* and cakes than I can count,"
Louis said, sharing the dream.

"Ah, to be home for Christmas!" said Jean-Paul.
"For *voyageurs* like us there is no Christmas," grumbled
Old Armand, stirring the thin fish soup on the fire. "We are a thousand
leagues away from anywhere. Père Noël does not come here."

"Are you sure of that?" A tall man stepped from the forest shadows into the light of the campfire. The voyageurs had never seen anyone like him, for he wore the clothes of another century.

"*Ma foi!*" Jean-Paul exclaimed. "One like that could have voyaged with La Salle!"

"Or Champlain!" Pascal whispered.

"Who are you?" Old Armand demanded to know.

"I have many names," the stranger said. He lifted the kettle and drank the steaming soup from the pot. "It needs more pepper."

"We have no pepper," Pascal replied.

"A poor way to spend Christmas," the stranger said.

"We make do with what we have." Pierre shrugged. "We are not in Montréal."

"Would you like to be?"

"In Montréal? This night? To celebrate Noël at home?"

"What do you want in return?" Old Armand asked warily.

"Nothing at all," the stranger replied. "I have been known to do a good deed from time to time, if only to amuse myself. Hear me, *mes amis*! I will return you to Montréal this night, on one condition: you may not speak a word until you reach your own homes."

"And if we speak?" Jean-Paul asked.

"Then you will come back here again. There is really nothing to lose."

Old Armand spat into the fire. "I know who you are, monsieur. We want none of your tricks. We will get home without your help, in God's good time."

"Armand! What are you saying?" the others cried. "To get home in one night? How can we refuse?"

Old Armand turned to the stranger. "My companions wish to accept your offer. I will go with them. What must we do?"

"Load your canoe and paddle home—as simple as that. But remember," the stranger reminded them, "no one must speak until he reaches his home. Do you agree?"

"We do," the voyageurs replied.

Old Armand whispered to the others, "This fellow is not as clever as he thinks. We can say what we like without speaking at all if we use the sign language of the Indians."

The voyageurs slid the canoe into the river and
took their places between bundles of baled furs.

"*Allez-vous-en, mes enfants!*" cried Old Armand.
The voyageurs dipped their paddles. The canoe rose
in the air. Faster and faster. Higher and higher. It skimmed
the treetops, skirting the clouds as it turned southward.

An ocean of stars lit the landscape below. The river shrank to a
silver thread. The lakes became fingers of ice.

Jean-Paul made signs to Étienne. He pointed out the marsh
where they had made a portage last summer. It took three days
to cross that dreadful place. It vanished into the distance
in less than a heartbeat.

The next few minutes found them flying over Lake Nipigon. Pascal made signs to Pierre. Pierre signed back that he recognized the island where they had found the blueberries. The juice had covered their hands and faces. They had looked like blue men.

Jean-Paul pointed over the side. Bear Cove lay below.

Louis shuddered, for he remembered the place where he had surprised an angry mother bear and her cubs. He had saved himself by pretending to be dead. Who could forget that adventure? he signed to Jean-Paul.

The canoe sped along. Each paddle stroke carried them ten leagues.

Étienne saw lights ahead. He signaled to Armand, who nodded. They had come to Fort Mackinac, the American fortress commanding the straits between Lake Huron and Lake Michigan.

The voyageurs saw two officers strutting across the parade ground. It would be fun to give them a Christmas present.

The voyageurs dipped their paddles. The canoe banked against a snow-covered rooftop. The officers shrieked as a blanket of snow slid down on their heads.

The canoe flew on. It passed through a blizzard. Covered in frost, the voyageurs looked like snowmen.

Louis peered through a blinding curtain of snow. What was that sound?

Étienne listened. It must be the falls of Niagara. They were over Lake Ontario—nearly home!

Old Armand brushed snowflakes from his eyes. Home. After so long.

The sky cleared. The stars lit their way up the Saint Lawrence River. The rooftops of Montréal came into view. The canoe sped over Pointe-à-Callière, dropping lower as it turned at the Place d'Armes. The copper steeple of Notre-Dame-de-Bon-Secours came into view.

They saw people filling the streets on their way to midnight Mass. The voyageurs recognized their loved ones. Étienne saw his wife, Yvette. Who was that boy walking with her? It must be Jacques, his son. How he had grown!

Jean-Paul saw his father. He looked so old. Where was Maman? She never missed Mass on Christmas Eve. His hands fell. He realized he would never see his mother again.

Pascal stared at a young woman walking beside a well-dressed man. She carried a sleeping baby. Faithless Marie! She had broken her promise. She had not waited for him.

Pierre clapped Pascal on the shoulder. His hands spoke. "What of it? You'll find another fiancée. The prettiest girls in the world live in Montréal."

Old Armand trembled with rage. He had just seen his youngest daughter walking with an officer from the fort. He had words to say, and he did not intend to sign them.

"Montmorency! You scoundrel! I warned you to stay away from Annette! I'm coming down to teach you a lesson!"

Another person suddenly appeared in the canoe.

"What a pity! You were almost home." He laughed. "Take a good look at Montréal. You won't be seeing it long."

"So you say," cried Old Armand with a mighty stroke. The canoe veered and stuck on the spire. It whirled around and around like a weather vane in a windstorm. The voyageurs and bales of fur slid down the chapel's roof to land safely in the snowdrifts. Shrieking with rage, the mysterious stranger streaked off toward the west.

Despite bruises and sore bones, all the voyageurs returned home for Christmas.
The furs they brought back made them wealthy men. Pascal found a new sweetheart, while
Old Armand made peace with Captain Montmorency, who married Annette that summer.

What became of the flying canoe? It spun around in wind and rain until it fell
apart. A piece of it is preserved in the Notre-Dame Basilica of Montréal to remind us
that miracles really do happen. Especially on Christmas Eve.

Author's Note

"The Flying Canoe," also known as "The Bewitched Canoe" (La Chasse-Galérie), is a French Canadian folktale whose origins go back to northern European legends of The Wild Hunt, which in turn has its roots in Norse mythology.

The many versions follow a similar pattern. A group of loggers or *voyageurs* are offered a chance to return home for one night, Christmas or New Year's Eve, on the condition that they do not speak or, in some versions, go near a church. The vow, of course, cannot be kept, and the travelers are whisked back to where they began—or to someplace worse. In most versions they travel in a canoe. In one, however, they ride on an ax handle that stretches to fit them all.

The best-known version of the story was written by Honoré Beaugrand and published in the August 1892 issue of *The Century Magazine*.

In 1991 Canada issued a postage stamp depicting the Bewitched Canoe. The legend was also commemorated at the opening ceremony for the 2010 Winter Olympics in Vancouver, B.C., as a canoe with fiddler Colin Maier descended from the ceiling.

Glossary

Noël: Christmas

Joyeux Noël: Merry Christmas

voyageurs: French Canadian traders who transported fur, supplies, and people across thousands of miles of wilderness in early Canada

Père Noël: Father Christmas, or Santa Claus

Ma foi!: By my faith!—A polite oath

René-Robert Cavelier, Sieur de La Salle: (1643–1687) An early French explorer whose expeditions included the Great Lakes region, the Mississippi River, and the Gulf of Mexico. In 1682 La Salle claimed the Mississippi River basin for France.

Samuel de Champlain: (1567–1635) The first of Canada's great explorers. In 1608 he established the settlement that became the city of Québec.

mes amis: my friends

Allez-vous-en, mes enfants!: Let's go, boys!

portage: A trip voyageurs made to carry goods from one body of water to another